My Summer Camp Diary!

by Stephanie Calmenson
illustrated by Nate Evans

Scholastic Inc.
New York Toronto London Auckland Sydney

To Amy Berkowitz,
who asked me to write this book.

Thanks to Amy Berkowitz, Dara Elovitch,
and Margo Ginsberg
for their expert readers' reports.

No part of this publication may be reproduced in whole or in part, or stored in a retrieval system, or transmitted in any form or by any means, electronic, mechanical, photocopying, recording, or otherwise, without written permission of the publisher. For information regarding permission, write to Scholastic Inc., 555 Broadway, New York, NY 10012.

ISBN 0-590-48398-6

Text copyright © 1995 by Stephanie Calmenson. Illustrations copyright © 1995 by Scholastic Inc. All rights reserved. Published by Scholastic Inc.

12 11 10 9 8 7   8 9/9 0/0

Printed in the U.S.A.   40

First Scholastic printng, May 1995

This Book Belongs to

_____

name

_____

age

_____

date

THIS IS ME BEFORE CAMP

Draw or paste your picture here.

WE'RE ON OUR WAY!

Summer camp begins as soon as you wave good-bye.

The name of my camp is _____

It is in _____, _____
        town   state

I got to camp by (circle one):

car   bus   train   airplane   boat   rocket ship

These are the people/animals who saw me off: _____

_____

When the ride started, I felt (check one or more):

☐   ☐   ☐   ☐   ☐ _____

excited   scared   happy   sad   fill in your own word

These are the kids I met on the way to camp: _____

_____

These are the kids I already knew: _____

_____

I sat next to _____

By the time I got to camp, I felt _____

MY FIRST DAY

Here are some important things to remember.

The Camp Director is: _____

My Head Counselor is: _____

My counselors are: _____, _____,

_____.

We live in: _____ _____.

          (write in)   (write in)

          tent, bunk,   name or

          cabin, other   number

My bunkmates are: _____

_____

_____

_____

My bed is next to: _____

I think camp is going to be (check one):

☐ fabulous   ☐ so-so

☐ wild   ☐ awful

☐ good   ☐ I don't know yet

Fabulous!

MY FIRST NIGHT

You got through it!

This is what we did on our first night: _____

_____

_____

_____

When the lights went out, I felt: _____

Check one:

- ☐ I fell asleep right away.
- ☐ I fell asleep soon.
- ☐ It took forever to fall asleep.

This was my dream. (Make one up if you don't remember.)

_____

_____

_____

_____

_____

I WANT TO GO HOME!

Everyone feels this way once in a while.

Things I miss:

- ☐ Warm showers
- ☐ Clean bathroom
- ☐ Comfortable bed
- ☐ Full refrigerator
- ☐ TV, music, remote control
- ☐ Air conditioner
- ☐ Everything I do not have here

People I miss most: _____

_____

Pets I miss: _____

Things I HATE so far:

- ☐ Yucky bathroom
- ☐ Uncomfortable bed
- ☐ Lumpy pillow
- ☐ No refrigerator
- ☐ No TV
- ☐ No air conditioner
- ☐ Mosquitoes!
- ☐ Other: _____

_____.

EW GROSS!

The food's not that bad—is it?

The worst foods here are: _____

_____

The foods I can swallow to avoid starvation are: ____

_____

The foods I actually like are: _____

_____

The foods I'll ask for second helpings of are: ____

_____

MUMMY!

Shh! In this game you are not allowed to talk.
How long can you last without saying anything?

As soon as you agree to play "Mummy," you are not allowed to talk. This is what happens each time you say a word:

First word . . . You lose your napkin.
                  (This is your warning.)

Second word . . . You lose your fork.
                  (You've still got your spoon.)

Third word . . . You lose your spoon.
                  (You've still got your knife.)

Fourth word . . . You lose your knife.
                  (Are your hands clean? You'll
                  need them!)

Fifth word . . . Hands behind your back, please.
                  (You've got to eat without your
                  hands? Oink, oink!)

Sixth word . . . You lose your chair and must eat
                  standing up.
                  (Have you noticed that everyone is
                  watching you?)

Seventh word . . . It's time to sit on the floor.
                  (Bye!)

FOOD, WAITER, WAITER!

Here's a song to sing
when your waiter or waitress is being a slowpoke.

Repeat from the beginning and keep singing until food
arrives. As you sing, beat out the rhythm on the table
this way:

F

We   want   some - thing   to   eat,   So

F

don't   fall   a - sleep   on   your   feet,   wait - er,   wait - er,

Food, wait - er, wait - er, wait - er, Food, wait - er, wait - er!

Food, wait - er, wait - er, wait - er, Food, wait - er, wait - er!

Here we sit like birds in the wil - der - ness,

Birds in the wil - der - ness, Birds in the wil - der - ness,

Here we sit like birds in the wil - der - ness,

Wait - ing for our food.

GOOPY, GREEN GOBBLERS

Can you finish this goopy story?

Do not read the story first.
On a piece of paper, write the numbers 1 to 12.
Fill in the words or names requested below.
Then read the story using your own words to fill in the blanks.

1. camper's name   2. a color   3. a food
4. descriptive word   5. descriptive word   6. camp name
7. a planet   8. a state   9. descriptive word
10. a number   11. descriptive word   12. a relative

One day, _____ sat down at the
₁

dining room table to eat lunch.

"Mmm. We're having _____ eggs,
₂

slippery _____, and _____
₃   ₄

bug juice."

"May we join you?" asked three _____
₅

creatures.

"Who are you?" asked _____.
₁

"We are the goopy, green gobblers of

_____," said the first creature.
₆

"Are you from _____ 7 ?" asked

_____ 1 .

"No. We are from _____ 8 . But we ate

the _____ 9 food here for

_____ 10 summers in a row," said the

second creature.

"And that is how we turned into goopy, green

gobblers!" said the third creature.

"Excuse me," said _____ 1 's waiter.

"Would you like any more of

our _____ 11

camp food?"

"No, thank you," said _____ 1 . "I am

full for the rest of the summer."

Then _____ 1 went back to the bunk to

write a letter home. This is what it said:

Dear _____ 12 ,

Please send a care package *fast*. Otherwise you may

never see me again. I will have turned into a goopy,

green gobbler!

_____ 1

PIG!

Keep one eye on your food and the other eye
on the kids at your table.

Here's how to play the game:

To start this game, one camper puts his index finger next
to his nose. Each camper who sees him holding up his
finger this way does the same thing.

The last camper to catch on — the one who does not
have his finger next to his nose when everyone else
does — is the pig.

Everyone points to that camper and sings:

When the song ends, the "pig" has to oink.
So pay attention—or you'll be the pig!

Oh, John - ny is a pi - ig, a pi - ig, a pi - ig. Oh, John - ny is a pi - ig, a pi - ig is he!

THE CANTEEN

It has everything you ever wanted.
Right?

Make a list of your favorite things sold at the canteen:

_____

_____

_____

_____

Make a list of the things you *wish* were sold at the canteen:

_____

_____

_____

_____

_____

_____

_____

_____

- Best friends
- Real shark
- Space ship
- Monster blood
- Robot back scratcher
- 1000-lb. candy bars
- love potions

THE LAKE

The big question is—
what's at the bottom?

Circle all the things you think are at the bottom of
your lake.

I'M TERRIFIC!

Here is your official summer camp activities chart.

For each activity, mark the column that describes you best by drawing a face in the box.

I like and am good at this.

I like this and I am okay.

I don't like this, but I am okay.

I got much better. I am terrific!

I don't like this and I am not good at all.

	I like and am good at this.	I like this and I am okay.	I don't like this, but I am okay.	I don't like this and I am not good at all.	I got much better. I am terrific!
Volleyball					
Swimming					
Sailing					
Canoeing					
Softball					
Basketball					
Tetherball					
Arts & Crafts					
Soccer					
Tennis					
_____					
_____					
_____					

DON'T FORGET TO WRITE!

The more letters you send, the more you get.
So start writing!

Here are some ideas to get you started writing letters.
Just copy these and fill in the blanks.

This one lets them know you are alive:

Dear _____,

   Hi. How are you?

   I am fine. Please write back soon.

          _____

This one lets them know you are alive and still thinking:

Dear _____,

   Hi. How are you?

   I am having a _____ time.

I really like _____.

There are some _____ kids here.

The food is pretty_____.

   Write back soon.

          _____

This one lets them know you are a cool camper:

Hey, _____
         dude/buddy/pal

    What's happenin'? This place is really

_____.

    You wouldn't believe the _____

here.

    Guess what! I am an excellent _____

_____. Amazing!

              Later _____

This letter may get you a few things.
Or, you will never hear from this person again:

Dearest _____,
              name of most generous
              person you know

    Camp is really great. I have most of
what I need. I am just missing a few
things. Maybe you could send them
sometime.

    Here's the list: _____, _____, _____,
                      food   food   food

_____,
                type of car

_____, _____, _____, _____,
  food   food   food   large sum of money

_____, _____, _____.
     food   food   food

    Thanks a bunch!

                    _____

DEAR DIARY

Write about the funniest thing that happened.

Date: _____

_____

_____

_____

_____

_____

_____

_____

_____

_____

_____

_____

_____

_____

DEAR DIARY

Write about the scariest thing that happened.

Date: _____

oooh!

Yikes

Aiiee!

Yow!

_____

_____

_____

_____

_____

_____

_____

_____

_____

_____

_____

DEAR DIARY

Write about the most romantic thing that happened.

Date: _____

DEAR DIARY

Write about the thing that made you so mad.

Date: _____

_____

_____

_____

_____

_____

_____

_____

_____

Arrgh!

Grrr!

rumble!

I hate that!

DEAR DIARY

Write about the thing that made you so proud.

Date: _____

_____

_____

_____

_____

_____

_____

_____

_____

_____

_____

DEAR DIARY

Write about your most embarrassing moment.

Date: _____

_____

_____

_____

_____

_____

_____

_____

_____

_____

DEAR DIARY

Write about a day you never want to forget.

Date: _____

_____

_____

_____

_____

_____

_____

_____

_____

_____

_____

_____

_____

_____

DEAR DIARY

Write about a day you wish you could forget.

Date: _____

_____

_____

_____

_____

_____

_____

_____

_____

_____

_____

_____

_____

_____

DEAR DIARY

Write about your biggest worry.

Date: _____

_____

_____

_____

_____

_____

_____

_____

_____

_____

_____

_____

_____

Oh no!

I know it's going to happen!

I can't take it!

DEAR DIARY

Write about how you feel to be going home.

Date: _____

_____

_____

_____

_____

_____

_____

_____

_____

_____

_____

_____

_____

SUMMER BOOKS

There is nothing better than reading a good book in the summertime.

Write down the title, author, and something you want to remember about each book you read.

1. _____

   _____

2. _____

   _____

3. _____

   _____

4. _____

   _____

5. _____

   _____

6. _____

   _____

SUMMER SONGS

Summer is a time for singing—
camp songs, pop songs, old songs, new songs.

These are the songs we sang all summer:

1. _____

   _____

2. _____

   _____

3. _____

   _____

4. _____

   _____

5. _____

   _____

6. _____

   _____

MY CAMP SONGS

Are there songs only your camp sings?
Write the words here.

_____
song title

_____

_____

_____

_____

_____

_____

_____

_____

_____

_____

_____

_____

_____

Write the words to your favorite
camp songs here.

_____
song title

_____

_____

_____

_____

_____

_____

_____

_____

_____

_____

_____

_____

_____

_____

_____

_____

_____

JOHN JACOB JINGLEHEIMER SCHMIDT

If you want to get where you're going in style,
try singing this song.

John Ja - cob Jing - le - heim - er

Schmidt. His name is my name

too. (God for - bid!) And when - ev - er we go

out, We can hear the peo - ple shout: "There goes

John Ja - cob Jing - le - heim - er

Schmidt." Dah, dah, dah, dah, dah, dah, dah.

dah, dah, dah, dah, dah. _____

Link arms with your friends and sing as you walk.
When you get to "dah, dah, dah . . . ," walk backwards.

Then begin the song again, walking forward again.
Sing it louder and louder each time, until you're
shouting it out.
On the last round, sing the song in a whisper,
then shout out, "DAH, DAH, DAH . . . !"

NUTS!

Want to drive anyone nuts? Sing this song.
It has no ending.

C   G

Boom, boom, ain't it great to be   cra - zy? Boom

C   G

boom, ain't it great to   be   nuts, like   us! Boom,

C   C7   F

boom, ain't it great to be   cra - zy?

G   C   G7

just   like   us. Boom, boom, boom,

WEB-FOOTED FRIENDS

Watch out.
This song has a trick ending.

Be kind to your web-foot-ed friends, For a

duck may be some-bod-y's moth - er. Be

kind to your friends in the swamp Where the

weath-er is al - ways damp You

may think that this is the end... *(spoken)* *Well, it is!*

THREE JOLLY FISHERMEN

This is a good bus song.
It's fun to sing and a little bit naughty.

The first one's name was Abraham.
The first one's name was Abraham.
Abra-Abra-ham-ham-ham.
Abra-Abra-ham-ham-ham.
The first one's name was Abraham!

The second one's name was I-Isaac.
The second one's name was I-Isaac.
I-I-saac-saac-saac.

I-I-saac-saac-saac.
The second one's name was I-Isaac.

The third one's name was Ja-a-cob.
The third one's name was Ja-a-cob.
Ja-a-cob-cob-cob.
Ja-a-cob-cob-cob.
The third one's name was Ja-a-cob.

They all went down to Amster-shh.
They all went down to Amster-shh.
Amster-Amster-shh-shh-shh.
Amster-Amster-shh-shh-shh.
They all went down to Amster-shh.

You mustn't say that naughty word.
You mustn't say that naughty word.
Naughty-naughty-word-word-word.
Naughty-naughty-word-word-word.
You mustn't say that naughty word.

I'm gonna say It anyhow.
I'm gonna say it anyhow.
Any-any-how-how-how.
Any-any-how-how-how.
I'm gonna say it anyhow.

They all went down to Amster-DAM!
They all went down to Amster-DAM!
Amster-Amster-DAM-DAM-DAM!
Amster-Amster-DAM-DAM-DAM!
They all went down to Amster-DAM!

OFFICIAL BUG BITE SCORECARD

Ouch! You can't escape them — bugs!

The next time you are bitten, fill in your bug bite scorecard. Compare bites with your friends. Who do the bugs love best?

Date of bite	Type of bug	Site of bite	Size of bump	Itchy or hurty

VISITING DAY

How was it? Tell all here.

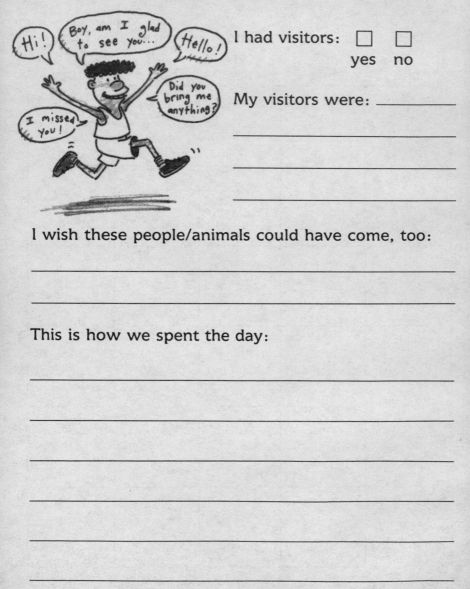

I had visitors: ☐ ☐
                      yes   no

My visitors were: _____

_____

_____

I wish these people/animals could have come, too:

_____

_____

This is how we spent the day:

_____

_____

_____

_____

_____

_____

48

My visitors brought me these things:

_____

_____

_____

I was so happy when: _____

_____

_____

_____

It really bothered me when: _____

_____

_____

_____

The day was: ☐ ☐ ☐
             great okay horrible

When my visitors left, I felt (check as many as you like):

☐ ☐ ☐ ☐ ☐
glad sad mad tired nauseous

☐ ☐ ☐
relieved homesick all of these

RAID!

What would camp be without 'em?

Raid Diary:

Date	Who raided whom	What happened on the raid
_____	_____	_____
_____	_____	_____
_____	_____	_____
_____	_____	_____
_____	_____	_____

Raiding Tips:

Always wear black when going on a raid. (Neon's a no-no.)

When going on a friendly raid, bring food!

Keep a comb and toothpaste under your pillow at night. If you are raided you want to look and feel your best.

DONUTS

WHERE'S MY OTHER SOCK?

And how about that favorite T-shirt?
And those pajama bottoms?

They call it "laundry." But everyone knows better.
The camp feeds your favorite clothes to a lean,
mean, clothes-eating machine!

Draw your missing items here.
It may be the closest you ever
get to seeing them again.

Socks!
Yum!

ACHOO!

Sprained ankle? Sore throat? Bee sting?
It's off to the infirmary!

SYMPTOM CHECKLIST
- ☐ Sore throat
- ☐ Temperature
- ☐ Cuts and bruises
- ☐ Broken bones
- ☐ Bellyache
- ☐ Faking it

TREATMENT
- ☐ Pat on the head
- ☐ Band-Aid
- ☐ Medicine
- ☐ Cast
- ☐ Kept overnight
- ☐ Trip to hospital

If you are kept overnight, this is big news.
Tell all here:

Who visited me: _____

Number of get well cards: _____

Number and kinds of presents: _____

Phone calls I got: _____

What I read: _____

_____

_____

SURVIVAL LIST

Oh, no! I forgot my boa constrictor!

Write down the things they forgot to tell
you to bring.
You'll want to remember them next summer.
(You are coming back next summer, aren't you?)

_____

_____

_____

_____

RAIN, RAIN, GO AWAY!

Some summers it rains more than others.

At camp, you will see movies at night.
You will also get to see lots of movies when it rains.
Write the names of the movies you see.
Rate them by checking the "Thumbs-up" or
"Thumbs-down" box.

Thumbs-up   Thumbs-down

☐ _____   ☐ _____

☐ _____   ☐ _____

☐ _____   ☐ _____

☐ _____   ☐ _____

☐ _____   ☐ _____

☐ _____   ☐ _____

☐ _____   ☐ _____

☐ _____   ☐ _____

CAMP WORD SEARCH PUZZLE

How about a puzzle to pass the time on a rainy day?
Look up, down, forwards, backwards, and diagonally
to find these hidden camp words:

soccer   infirmary   flag   tennis   bee
mail call   swim   mosquito   bug   canteen
oars   tent   lake   mud   campfire   raid

```
T  Y  R  A  M  R  I  F  N  I
N  K  M  S  T  T  G  A  L  F
E  S  O  C  C  E  R  B  M  V
T  J  S  K  A  N  E  U  A  Z
R  L  Q  G  N  N  D  N  I  G
M  A  U  B  T  I  I  K  L  U
I  K  I  B  E  S  P  A  C  B
W  E  T  D  E  Q  S  R  A  O
S  Q  O  J  N  E  U  T  L  X
E  R  I  F  P  M  A  C  L  P
```

REST HOUR

It's time for reading, writing,
dozing, and puzzling.

GET BUSY!

Use the clues to fill in this crossword puzzle.
The answers are all things you can do when rest
hour is over.

Across

2. Put on your bathing suit and go _____.

3. Get a bow and arrow for _____.

6. Rehearse for a _____.

8. Swing your _____ in a game of softball.

10. Hit the ball with any part of your body except
your arms or hands in a game of _____.

Down

1. Get out your boots and backpack to go on
a _____.

4. Make something great in arts and _____.

5. Grab those oars and _____ that boat.

7. Reach the finish line as fast as you can in a _____.

9. Hit a volleyball over the _____.

BIRDS, BEES, SKY, TREES

Sometimes its nice just to stop and smell the flowers.

Sit by yourself on the grass — think, read, watch the clouds go by. Here are a few poems to keep you company.

I'M GLAD THE SKY

I'm glad the sky is painted blue,
   And the earth is painted green,
With such a lot of nice fresh air
   All sandwiched in between.

Author unknown

THE CROCUS

The golden crocus reaches up
To catch a sunbeam in her cup.

Walter Crane

CLOUDS

White sheep, white sheep,
On a blue hill,
When the wind stops
You all stand still.
When the wind blows
You walk away slow.
White sheep, white sheep,
Where do you go?

Christina Rossetti

What do you see? What are you thinking of? Draw a picture or write a poem here.

THERE'S AN ELEPHANT IN MY BUNK!

Here are some silly summer riddles to amuse you.

CAMP CRITTERS

How can you tell if there's an elephant in your bunk?
You can smell the peanuts on his breath.

Who joined the campers when they were singing in the woods?
The Bear-itones.

Why didn't the camper run when he saw a bear?
He didn't want a bear behind.

Why did the skunk tiptoe past the campers?
He didn't want to wake the sleeping bags.

Which animals annoy campers most?
Badgers.

CAMPER NEWS

What happened to the camper who swallowed a flashlight?
She hiccupped with delight.

What is easy for a camper to get into, but hard to get out of?
Trouble.

If a camper gets into trouble, what can she always count on?
Her fingers.

Should a camper ever go sailing on a full stomach?
No. She should always go sailing on water.

If there are 99 campers on a boat and the boat turns over, how many campers will there be?
66.

GOING BUGGY

What bees are hard to talk to?
Mumble bees.

What insect flies, bites, and wears dark glasses?
A mosquito working undercover.

How do you start a flea race?
You say, "One, two, *flea,* go!"

How do you start a firefly race?
You say, "One, two, three, *glow*!"

Why couldn't the firefly remember the words to the camp cheer?
He wasn't very bright.

Which bugs are not allowed in a boys' camp?
Ladybugs.

HOMEWARD BOUND

What did the mother frog say when her tadpole came home from camp?
"I'm hoppy to see you!"

What campers take a bus home?
None. A bus is too heavy to carry.

What is gray with four legs and a trunk?
A mouse going to camp.

What is red with four legs and a trunk?
A sunburned mouse coming back from camp.

Why did Humpty Dumpty have a great fall?
Hey, why not? He had a great summer!

HA-HA!

Here's a silly game to play during free time.
Try not to laugh!

Here is how to play:
Everyone lies on the ground, as shown.
The first camper says, "Ha!"
The next camper says, "Ha-ha!"
The third camper says, "Ha-ha-ha!"
And so on.

The object of the game is to keep a straight
face and not burst out laughing.
The last one to laugh is the winner.
(Usually everyone breaks up laughing and
nobody wins this game.)

I WENT TO THE STORE

Here is another game that can get pretty silly.
This time you can laugh all you want.

Here is how to play:
The leader makes up a story with actions.
Each player copies the actions of the leader.
Once an action is introduced, players must continue
it throughout the game, so that hands, feet, head,
and so on are all in motion at once.
Whoever keeps doing the actions the longest wins.
Here is an example:

Leader: I went to the toy store.
Outside there was a gum machine.
I bought a piece of gum.
(Action: Chewing gum)

Leader: Then I went inside to buy a jump rope.
(Action: Chewing and jumping rope)

Leader: While I was going down the aisle, I
stubbed my toe.
*(Action: Chewing, jumping, and hopping up and
down)*

Leader: The next thing I knew, someone was
calling my name. I turned around to see
who it was.
*(Action: Chewing, jumping, hopping, and turning
round and round)*

Leader: The store manager wanted to know if I needed any help. I shook my head no.

(Action: Chewing, jumping, hopping, turning, and shaking head)

To play the game just for fun, with no winner, here is a good way to end:

Leader: I found the jump rope and bought it. I jumped all the way home. Then I went to sleep.

(Action: Lying on floor, sleeping)

MY BUNK

It's the best!

AND THE WINNER IS . . .

Here are some awards for your bunkmates.
Write the name of each winner on the lines below.

The Messiest Camper Award goes to _____

The Funniest Camper Award goes to _____

The Most Athletic Camper Award goes to _____

The Laziest Camper Award goes to _____

The Bravest Camper Award goes to _____

The Whiniest Camper Award goes to _____

The Most Talkative Camper Award goes to _____

Fill in your own awards here:

_____

_____

_____

ONE FOR ALL AND ALL FOR ONE!

Check off the things you and your bunkmates have done to let the rest of the world know who you are.

☐ Put clothes on backwards

☐ Had breakfast in pajamas

☐ Walked into the dining hall backwards

☐ Dressed in the same color

☐ Wore hats

☐ _____

☐ _____

☐ _____

OH COUNSELOR, MY COUNSELOR!

Does this fill-in story describe *your* counselor?

Do not read the story yet.
On a piece of paper, write the numbers 1 to 17.
Fill in the words or names requested below.
Then read the story using your own words to fill in the blanks.

1. your counselor's name   2. descriptive word
3. a color   4. a number   5. another number
6. object (plural)   7. object (singular)
8. camp name   9. descriptive word
10. descriptive word   11. your name
12. another camper's name   13. an animal
14. something found in the bathroom
15. something found in a drugstore
16. descriptive word   17. an animal

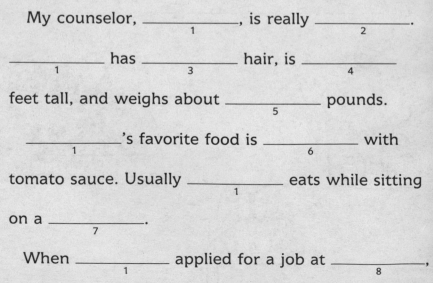

My counselor, _____, is really _____.
            1   2

_____ has _____ hair, is _____
   1   3   4

feet tall, and weighs about _____ pounds.
                                   5

_____'s favorite food is _____ with
     1   6

tomato sauce. Usually _____ eats while sitting
                          1

on a _____.
      7

When _____ applied for a job at _____,
       1   8

they said, "You're hired! Your campers will be

_____ and _____. They will need to be
　　　9　　　　　　　　10

watched closely, especially _____ and _____.
　　　　　　　　　　　　　　11　　　　　　　12

Please bring a(n) _____, a(n) _____, and
　　　　　　　　　13　　　　　　　　14

a(n) _____."
　　　15

　　We all think _____ is a _____ counselor.
　　　　　　　　　1　　　　　　　16

We would not trade _____ for any other
　　　　　　　　　　　1

_____ in the whole world!
　　17

Draw
a picture
of your
counselor
here.

AROUND THE CAMPFIRE

Cozy? Spooky? Buggy? Fun?
Or all of the above?

Some kids love campfires. Some kids hate 'em. Either way, it will be fun to look back at them someday.

What we ate:

_____

_____

I ☐   ☐   get a bellyache.
 did did not

These are the bugs
and animals I saw (or was eaten by):

☐ Bears   ☐ Mosquitoes   ☐ Ants   ☐ Raccoons

☐ Bats   ☐ Rabbits   ☐ Fireflies

_____   _____   _____

A campfire is the place for singing and storytelling:

Stories we told:

_____

_____

_____

_____

Songs we sang:

_____

_____

_____

_____

I would like to have campfires:

☐ Every day   ☐ Once a week   ☐ Once a month

☐ Once a year   ☐ Maybe in my
                              next life

BOO!

Tell these spooky stories at a campfire
or when the lights are out.

IN A DARK, DARK SUMMER CAMP

Here is a variation on the old favorite, "In a Dark, Dark House." The leader chants each line in a voice that gets spookier and spookier. The rest of the group repeats each line the same way after the leader. At the end, everyone shouts together, "Boo!"

In a dark, dark summer camp
There's a dark, dark bunk.
In the dark, dark bunk
There's a dark, dark cubby.
In the dark, dark cubby,
There's a dark, dark shelf.
On the dark, dark shelf
There's a dark, dark knapsack.
In the dark, dark knapsack,
There's a GHOST!
BOO!

If you want to make this even sillier, just keep the story going with silly places and silly things.

WHO'S GOT MY HAIRY TOE?

Do *you* have the hairy toe?

One day a man went out to his garden to pick some beans and found a big, hairy toe. He took the toe home and cooked it and ate it for supper.

That night when he went to bed, he could hear the wind howling through the trees. Suddenly the door to his house blew open with a bang! A voice in the dark cried, "Who's got my hairy toe?"

Clunk. Clunk. The man heard footsteps coming towards his room.

The voice wailed, "Who's got my hairy toe?"

Clunk. Clunk. The footsteps were getting closer. The voice was getting louder. "Who's got my hairy toe?"

Creak. The door to the bedroom opened.

"Who's got my hairy toe?" groaned the voice.

Clunk. Clunk. Clunk. Footsteps stopped at the man's bedside. The creature leaned over the man's bed and shouted, *"YOU'VE GOT IT!"*

(Jump at the person next to you when you shout out the last line.)

The hairy toe ← (gross!)

THE VIPER IS COMING

The more floors you add, the scarier this story gets!

It was a dark and gloomy afternoon. A lady was all alone in her apartment on the top floor of her building. Sudddenly the telephone rang. The lady jumped up to answer it.

"It's the viper," said a strange voice. "I'm coming to see you."

Click. The phone went dead. The lady was scared. She fell into her chair to think. The phone rang again. The lady jumped up to answer it.

"It's the viper," said the voice. "I'm on the first floor."

Click. The phone went dead. The lady was trembling. What was she going to do? Before she knew it, the phone rang again.

"It's the viper," said the voice. "I'm on the second floor."

Click. The phone went dead. The lady needed a plan. But she was so scared, her brain went numb. The phone rang again.

"It's the viper," said the strange voice. "I'm on the third floor."

Click. The phone went dead. The lady could hardly breathe, she was so scared. The viper had one more floor to go. Who could help the lady now?

Then came the knock at her door. The lady screamed. She opened the door a crack.

A man carrying a bucket and rags poked his head inside. "I'm the viper!" he said. "I've come to vipe your vindows!"
(*The last line is spoken in a cheerful voice.*)

THE GHOST WITH
THE BLOODY FINGER

Would you take pity on a poor ghost?

On a hot summer afternoon, a hiker passed an eerie old house. From inside she heard a voice cry, *"I have a bloody finger. Help me!"*

"Who are you? How can I help?" called the hiker.

"Come closer and I will tell you," wailed the voice.

The hiker was afraid, but she could not ignore someone in need. She opened the door to the house and went inside. It was so dark and she could hardly see. She brushed spiderwebs from her face and hair. Then she heard the voice again, crying for help.

"Where are you?" asked the hiker.

"I'm up in the attic," the voice wailed. *"I have a bloody finger. Ooh!"*

The hiker climbed the broken steps to the second floor.

"Help me! Help me!" wailed the voice.

She climbed to the third floor. Something in the air made her shiver.

"Hurry. Hurry!" cried the voice.

The air grew colder with every step the hiker took. But she kept climbing. Finally she reached the attic and threw open the door. The hiker screamed. "Ahhhh!"

A bloody finger was floating in the air. It floated up to the hiker's face.

"Wh-wh-what do you want from me?" the hiker cried.

"I am the ghost with the bloody finger. Could you give me a Band-Aid, please?"

THE YELLOW RIBBON

Why does the girl wear a yellow ribbon around her neck?

A boy and a girl lived next door to each other. They went to school and played together all the time. They liked each other very much and knew each other well.

But there was one thing the boy did not understand. The girl always wore a yellow ribbon around her neck. She was never without it.

"Why do you wear that ribbon around your neck all the time?" asked the boy.

"I can't tell you now," said the girl. "Maybe someday I will."

Years passed. The boy and girl grew up. They fell in love and they married. Still, the young woman never took off her yellow ribbon.

yellow
ribbon

"Now that we are married, won't you tell me why you wear the ribbon?" asked the young man.

"I can't tell you," said the young woman. "Maybe someday I will."

Their lives together were happy. They worked, and raised a family. From time to time the man would ask his wife why she wore the yellow ribbon.

"We are happy together, aren't we? So what difference does it make?" asked the wife.

"I just want to know is all," said the husband.

"I can't tell you yet," said the wife. "Maybe someday I will."

More time passed. The man and woman grew old together. Through good times and bad, they liked and loved each other as they always had.

Then one day the woman grew very ill. She was close to dying.

The man knelt at her bedside and sobbed. In the little time that was left to them, they talked of their good life together. Then the man asked, "Can you tell me now why you wear a yellow ribbon around your neck?"

The woman sighed.

"I guess it is time for you to know," she said. "Untie the ribbon and your question will be answered."

The man gently pulled one end of the ribbon. When it came undone . . .

Plop! The woman's head fell off.

CAMP TRIPS

You might want to have a record of your camp trips. Then, again, you might not. You decide.

Date: _____

Where we went: _____

My trip buddy: _____

Souvenirs: _____

I had a ☐ ☐ ☐ time.
    good bad so-so

Date: _____

Where we went: _____

My trip buddy: _____

Souvenirs: _____

I had a ☐ ☐ ☐ time.
    good bad so-so

Date: _____

Where we went: _____

My trip buddy: _____

Souvenirs: _____

I had a ☐ ☐ ☐ time.
     good bad so-so

SPECIAL EVENTS

How about those campfires, socials, treasure hunts?
Were they fun, or a bummer?

Your counselors worked hard to plan them. The least
you can do is remember them.

Date: _____

Special event: _____

I had a ☐ ☐ ☐ time.
    good bad so-so

Date: _____

Special event: _____

I had a ☐ ☐ ☐ time.
    good bad so-so

Date: _____

Special event: _____

I had a ☐ ☐ ☐ time.
    good bad so-so

IT'S SHOW TIME!

Not everyone can be the star.
But everyone's part is important.

Name of the play: _____

The stars were: _____

This was my contribution to the play:

☐ Star   ☐ Co-star   ☐ Big part

☐ Small part   ☐ Understudy   ☐ Lights

☐ Stagehand   ☐ Set design   ☐ Costumes

☐ Musician   ☐ Floor mopper   ☐ Troublemaker

Draw a picture from the play here.

YAY, TEAM!

Color War. Camp Olympics. Intercamp Games.
There are lots of times when you'll need a good cheer.

Our team is red hot!
Your team is didilly squat.

Side out and rotate!
Our team is really great!

Our team is red hot!
Your team is all shot. (Bang, bang!)

Our team is red hot.
Your team is green snot. (Achoo!)

This is a good cheer for anyone,
especially your faithful bus driver.

2 - 4 - 6 - 8,
Who do we appreciate?
The bus driver! The bus driver!
Hooray!

If your camp has Color War, Camp Olympics, or any other major camp competition, fill in the lines below:

How it broke: _____

_____

Name of teams: _____ and _____.

My team: _____

I ☐   ☐   on the same team as my best friend(s).
  was   was not

Our team song was called: _____.

The winning team was: _____.

I ☐   ☐   ☐   this whole thing.
  liked   did not mind   hated

I DON'T WANT TO GO HOME

When the end gets near,
the countdown begins.

Ten more days of va - ca - tion,

Then it's time for the sta - tion.

Back to civ - i - li - za - tion!

I don't want to go home.

I don't want to go home.

I don't want to go home.

Nine more days of vacation . . .
and so on until
No more days of vacation,
Now it's time for the station,
Back to civilization—
I don't want to go home!

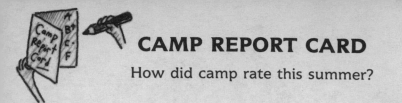

CAMP REPORT CARD

How did camp rate this summer?

Tell it all in your own words.

Camp Director: _____

Head Counselor: _____

Counselor #1: _____

Counselor #2: _____

Counselor #3: _____

Kids in bunk: _____

Activities: _____

Food: _____

Weather: _____

Bugs: _____

Members of
the opposite sex: _____

Would you go back to the same camp next year?

☐ yes   ☐ no   ☐ maybe

PICTURE PAGE

They say a picture
is worth a thousand words.

Draw or paste pictures of your camp friends here.

FRIENDS WE ARE, FRIENDS WE'LL BE

On these pages clean and bright,
ask your friends if they will write.

KEEP IN TOUCH

If you're lucky, the friends you make at camp
will be friends for life.

Name: _____
Address: _____
Phone Number: _____

Name: _____
Address: _____
Phone Number: _____

Name: _____
Address: _____
Phone Number: _____

Name: _____
Address: _____
Phone Number: _____

Name: _____
Address: _____
Phone Number: _____

Name: _____

Address: _____

Phone Number: _____

Name: _____

Address: _____

Phone Number: _____

Name: _____

Address: _____

Phone Number: _____

Name: _____

Address: _____

Phone Number: _____

Name: _____

Address: _____

Phone Number: _____

Name: _____

Address: _____

Phone Number: _____

THIS IS ME AFTER CAMP

Draw or paste your picture here.